For Kate

Have you read these picture books by Emma Chichester Clark?

I Love You, Blue Kangaroo!

Where Are You, Blue Kangaroo?

It Was You, Blue Kangaroo!

What Shall We Do, Blue Kangaroo?

I'll Show You, Blue Kangaroo!

Merry Christmas, Blue Kangaroo!

Happy Birthday, Blue Kangaroo!

With thanks to Quentin Blake for his kind permission in allowing
The Dancing Frog to make an appearance in this book.

First published in hardback in Great Britain
by HarperCollins Children's Books in 2012

1 3 5 7 9 10 8 6 4 2

ISBN: 978-0-00-725867-3

Visit our website at www.harpercollins.co.uk

Printed in China

Blue Kangaroo belonged to Lily.
He was her very own kangaroo.
One day, Lily told him that she had to go to a new school.
She looked into his eyes and said, "Will you come too,
Blue Kangaroo?" And Blue Kangaroo thought, "Yes!" and
smiled his secret smile.

Lily had to get new pencils and a new school bag. Her mother made a little bag for Blue Kangaroo and tied it round his tummy.

"I don't think he wants to go to
the new school," said Lily.
"But there'll be lots of fun
things to do," said her mother.

Blue Kangaroo liked
the sound of that.

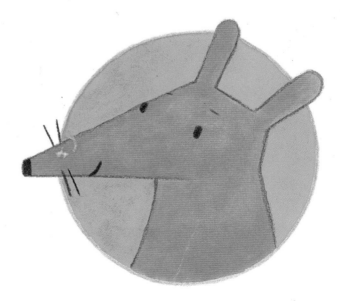

Aunt Jemima brought Lily a new lunch box to put her
sandwiches in and a tiny box of raisins for Blue Kangaroo.

"He's a bit scared about the new school," said Lily.
Aunt Jemima smiled at Blue Kangaroo. "New things can be a bit scary," she said, "but he won't be new for long, and he'll make lots of friends."

Blue Kangaroo thought he might really like new things.

Aunt Florence came with a new pencil case for Lily and a tiny packet of pencils for Blue Kangaroo.

"He's worried about getting lost
at the new school," said Lily.
"But there'll be lots of people
there to help him find
everything," said Aunt Florence.

Blue Kangaroo wanted to go
and explore the new school
right away!

The next day, Lily's mother took Lily to the new school.
Her friends, Talullah and Milly, were there. They were
new too. They waved at Lily.

"Wait!" cried Lily. "I think Blue Kangaroo has a tummy ache! He wants to go home!"
"Oh, dear," said Lily's mother. "Let's find your teacher – she'll know what to do."

The teacher smiled at Lily and Blue Kangaroo. "Hallo, Lily," she said. "I'm Miss Zazou."

"Hallo, Miss Zazou," said Lily. "I'm worried about my Blue Kangaroo."

Miss Zazou looked at Blue Kangaroo. "He is so lucky,"
she said, "to have you to look after him on his first day
at a new school."
Then she showed Lily where to put her coat.

In the classroom, Miss Zazou showed Lily where to sit and she put Blue Kangaroo on the windowsill so he could watch. First everyone drew shapes and coloured them.

After that, they did numbers.
"What do you get if you
add four and two?" asked
Miss Zazou.
Lily put up her hand.

Blue Kangaroo smiled.
He knew that one too.

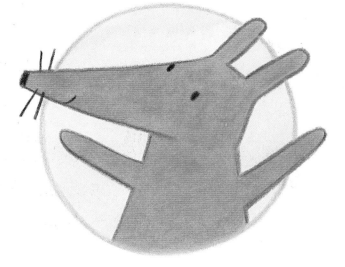

At break time, all of Lily's class went to the playground.
They played with hoops and ran around.

Then they had juice and biscuits.
Blue Kangaroo watched Lily. She was *really* having fun.

All day, Blue Kangaroo sat on the windowsill, watching. There was painting and sticking and there was building things with wooden blocks.

"I wish, I wish I could do it too," thought Blue Kangaroo.

And then it was story time. The children sat on cushions in the reading corner and listened to a story about a dancing frog.

When it was time to go, Lily's mother was there. Lily had
so many things to tell her, she didn't stop talking, all the
way home.

Everyone wanted to know about Lily's first day at her
new school.
"And what about Blue Kangaroo?" asked Aunt Jemima.
"Oh, no!" cried Lily. "I've forgotten him!"

"Please, Mummy, can we go and get Blue Kangaroo?"
"Oh, Lily," said her mother. "The school will be closed
now. But don't worry – Blue Kangaroo will be all right –
he'll be there waiting for you in the morning."

Blue Kangaroo sat alone in the classroom.
At first, he felt sad about being forgotten. But then he
thought, "Now I can do all the things that Lily did today!"

Blue Kangaroo jumped down from the windowsill.

He began by drawing his favourite shapes and colouring them.

Then he got out the building blocks and built some tall towers.

Next he painted pictures
of all the children

and did all the sums
he knew on the
white board.

And then he made flower
pictures with glue and sparkles
that glittered in the moonlight.

While he was working, he remembered the story Miss
Zazou had read about the dancing frog. Blue Kangaroo
hopped over to the reading corner and looked at
the pictures.

Soon he began to feel sleepy. He didn't want to be too
tired for school the next day, so he curled up on a cushion
and fell fast asleep. The sooner he went to sleep, the sooner
he would see Lily.

In the morning, Lily rushed to school. Miss Zazou was
in the classroom with the Head Teacher.
"It's amazing!" said Miss Zazou.

"Who could have done it?" asked the Head Teacher.
Lily had spotted Blue Kangaroo lying on the cushion.
"I know who did it," she whispered, as she hugged him tight.

Blue Kangaroo spent the day on the windowsill again, watching Lily learn new things. She was very busy but she and Miss Zazou kept an eye on Blue Kangaroo to make sure he was happy.

At the end of the day, Lily went
to say goodbye to Miss Zazou.
"See you tomorrow, Miss Zazou,"
she said.
"Will you come too, Blue
Kangaroo?" asked Miss Zazou.

"Oh, yes!" thought Blue
Kangaroo. "I'm coming too!"

Before Lily went to bed, she put out some paper and pencils
for Blue Kangaroo.
"I'm looking forward to school tomorrow!" she said.
Blue Kangaroo smiled his secret smile.
He was too!